This book belongs to

To Ken, Alexis, and Olivia, with love.
—C.T-B.

To my Mother, who loves ponies.
—M.M.

Library of Congress Cataloging-in-Publication Data is available.

4 6 8 10 9 7 5 3

Published by Sterling Publishing Co. Inc., 387 Park Avenue South, New York, NY 10016

Designed and produced for Sterling by COLOR-BRIDGE BOOKS, LLC, Brooklyn, NY

Distributed in Canada by Sterling Publishing
c/o Canadian Manda Group, 165 Dufferin Street
Toronto, Ontario, Canada M6K 3H6
Distributed in Great Britain and Europe by Chris Lloyd at Orca Book Services
Stanley House, Fleets Lane, Poole BH15 3AJ, England
Distributed in Australia by Capricorn Link (Australia) Pty. Ltd.
P.O. Box 704, Windsor, NSW 2756, Australia

Printed in China

Sterling ISBN 1-4027-2018-1

A Pony to Love

by Christine Taylor-Butler
Illustrated by Mary Morgan

Sterling Publishing Co., Inc.
New York

I'm your own special pony.
Let's play outside.
Together we'll go
on a magical ride. . . .

Mount my saddle.
Hold my reins tight.

We ponies are gentle
and very polite!

So many adventures await you and me.
We can prance on the beach.
We can splash in the sea!

We can gallop through fields
of tall prairie flowers.

Then we'll race to the mountains—
our ride lasts for hours!

We can stop for a rest
by a country lane,
and you can braid ribbons
through my silky mane.

Look—see the apples!
One for you. One for me.
Our ride made me hungry.
I think I'll eat three.

Now off to the Big Top
with three circus rings.

We'll fly through the hoops
as if we had wings.

In winter we'll gallop
through new fallen snow.
Then we'll snuggle up warm
when the arctic winds blow.

We can trot down the street
in a grand parade.
Wave to the people!
Don't be afraid!

Let's try for a prize at the rodeo.
If we take five blue ribbons,
we win "Best of Show"!

Feed me some grain
and a carrot or two.
Brush my coat
till it's shiny and new.

With a pony to love,
you can't go wrong.
Right by your side
is where I belong.